ERROR

YOU ARE FAR MORE ANNOYING THAN
WHAT I'VE HEARD.

AARCHI ADVANI SAINI

ISBN 979-888546984-5

Contents

Author

Aarchi Advani Saini.!
    [ ] Author of the book "The Loads Of Poetry"
[ ] Social media "Aarchi Advani Saini"
[ ] Aries, believe in destiny.

Aarchi Advani Saini.!

[ ] Author of the book "The Loads Of Poetry Part One and Two", "The Journey of Love", "The Way to Love", "The Anonymous", "Let's be Confidante", "The Cabalistic Child ", "Confession", "Dark Dead", "Faith is All", "The Street of Paris", "It's All About Destiny", "Half Dead", and more.

She becomes one of the youngest author of her hometown Shamli. For This Danik Jagran's newspaper covers this news, Later, many news channels interviewed her. So renowned for "The loads of poetry). She has sold the book worldwide, the recipient of numerous prestigious awards in her writing journey. She writes daily columns syndicated throughout the world. Aarchi Advani is well known for her writing on many other platforms. She is also a fantasy and literary fiction author specializing in "Life", as well as her upcoming book "Lifeless Life."

She publish her 10th book as her Hindi novel called "papa".

She also hosts a channel where she uses her passion for storytelling. And a background in business to help other creatives navigate their writing. So she is compiling an anthology named, "Of Your Choice", And her publishing journey is another level, she is good at her writing skills, but no one knows how to write books, same with her, but with the passage of time, she grows. When she's not writing or tubing she enjoys listening to books,

Making stories on her own. And love to live in her virtual world.

CHAPTER ONE

Self-Appreciation

Self-Appreciation is important, As you can't always depends on others to be appreciated. Be the first to flaunt yourself.
Aarchi Advani Saini.!
A beautiful Monday morning, the sun rays kissed her cheeks and the birds chirping outside in a chorus to wake her up. The sky is clear and sun is sparkling bright. Her mom enters her room and pulls out her blanket as she is hidden inside it.
Mom - get up beta! Do you wanna be late today as well. There's no use opening the window and switching off the fan ! You still won't get up. Dr. Lazy get up! Error.!
Kaira - (in a sleepy tone) five minutes maa , pleasshhh,
Mom - its please and it's 8:30AM get up !
Kaira - oh shit , (she said in panic , but her face was calm , she yawned)
Mom - place your hand on your mouth. ugh!
Kaira - good morning my jaan (my life)
Mom - you are getting late ! Hurry up .
Kaira - maa , don't you know good things take time to happen , they are always late. And me , I'm not just the good thing , I'm the best thing. (She flips her long hair)

Mom - don't you get tired by appreciating yourself so much.
Kaira - there is nothing to be tired of maa. You can't always depend on others to appreciate you, sometimes you need to tap your shoulder yourself.
Mom - enough of philosophy, now get ready.

———————————

She gets ready for her college ,her hair, naturally brown tied up in a high ponytail , face so serene , lips like rose kissed , her cheeks pink enough and a smile with dimples , that can heal anyone. She reaches the college and bangs on the shoulder of her best friend,
Aarohi. They know each other since childhood. As kaira is a fatherless and only child , she'd spend most of her time with Aarohi.
Aarohi - aahhhh! I'll surely die one day because of you.
Kaira - don't worry , I'll be with you too.
Aarohi - Kaira! (She exclaimed) did you do something yesterday?
Kaira - what ? Nothing (she looked away) what are you talking about?
Aarohi - you know what I'm talking about.
Kaira - (maintains to be silent, enter the classroom) good morning people (loud enough)
(All the students greeted kaira. Being the most notorious student of the school she is known by every one and loved to.)
The teacher enters and faces Kaira.
Teacher - Ms. Kaira , can you explain me why have you placed fire crackers behind Arun yesterday.
Kaira - oh! that's the case , you scared me with your facial expressions.
Teacher - raised her eyebrows at her.

Kaira - ma'am actually he was flirting around with every girl, calling them with disgusting names like item, bomb , pataka(fire cracker) etc etc. So I just wanted him to know how exactly it feels when the so called fire crackers are actually behind you.

(All the students laughing)

Maam - silence! Are you crazy Kaira ! Anything would have happened to him , will you take the blame.

Kaira - don't worry maam , I've taken Al the necessary precautions before I did this crap.

Teacher - what have your mom eaten before your birth , why are you soo.....

Kaira - basically she had eaten food. Specifically, I don't know because I was inside the tummy, I'll ask her and let you know. But tamarind most of all.

Teacher - Kaira aaaa!!!!!

CHAPTER TWO

Mowgli

Guys, look cute with messy hair, but with long hair, they look like a Mowgli. Sleeves rolled up to elbows, haye, killer.

Aarchi Advani Saini.!

Another teacher appears. Kaira greets her, Good morning Mrs. Khan.

Mrs. Khan - Good morning, Kaira, what I've been hearing about you is true.

Kaira - Absolutely ma'am, there is no one in the college who dares to spread rumors about Kaira. So whatever you will hear it will be true.

Mrs. Khan - can you be serious for some time.

Kaira - sure! She straightens her face and makes a stern expression.

Mrs. Khan - (laughing) what are you doing?

Kaira - being serious.

Teacher - stop it both of you! What's wrong. And you Mrs. Khan I've called you here to scold this brat.

Kaira - who brat, ??¿¿ (points her finger at herself) this innocent soul looks like a brat, (she frowns)

Teacher - started her drama again! What kind of Doctor you are Kaira?

Kaira - A cute, little, innocent, and annoying doctor. *flips her hair*

Mrs. Khan - anyways, everyone line up we are leaving for the practical test, it's the part of your internship, get ready.

Teacher - what about Arun Mrs. Khan?

Kaira - chapter close. *showing all her teeth* error.!

Everybody sits inside the bus while Kaira starts to sing songs. All the students joined her. They reached the CITY CENTRAL HOSPITAL, well known for all specialists.

Mrs. Khan - my dear students you all will be attending a welcome speech from a well-known cardiologist Dr. Kabir, he is the youngest surgeon here. He will be your mentor and your leader too. Don't annoy him, especially you Dr. Kaira. Are you listening?

Kaira - yes ma'am, I won't annoy him (whispers to Aarohi, because I'm gonna irritate him)

Mrs. Khan - Dr. Kaira your whispers are loud enough to be heard, but I request you not to do any crap here.

Kaira - sure.

(All the students went inside the hospital and gathered in a room waiting for Dr.
Kabir to arrive.)

Nurse - please be seated here, Dr. Kabir will be attending you all soon. He is busy with surgery.

All the students settled down, meanwhile, Kaira disappeared.

Aarohi - hey, where Kaira guys?

Everybody looked out for her and
Dr. Kabir entered.

A muscular man with a white formal shirt, sleeves raised to elbows, hairs messy yet neat, eyes, wood brown.

ERROR

Kabir - welcome to CITY CENTRAL HOSPITAL, interns. I hope you all are doing great and are really passionate about your work. (he continued his speech. The door opens and Kaira sneaks in. Hides behind the nurses standing near the wall and reaches her seat.)

Kaira - huh! Did I miss anything? Dayummmmmm, he looks hot Aaru! Guys look cute with messy hair but with long hair, they look like a Mowgli. And sleeves rolled up to elbows, haye, killer.

Aarohi - ssshhh.... focus on his words, he is looking at you.

Kaira - (sets her hair) really?

Aarohi - shut up!

Kabir - Dr. Kaira, indeed you've missed a lot.

Kaira - (silent)

Kabir - can I ask you where were you?

Kaira - canteen

Kabir - why? Didn't you have your breakfast?

Kaira - nope, I woke up late and I didn't eat. And the samosas of your canteen smelled good but tasted oily, (she turns to the nurse) ask the cook to use less oil.

Kabir - I hope you won't leave your patient for a samosa.

Kaira - hopefully.

Kabir - (makes an annoyed expression) You are far more annoying than what I've heard.

Kaira - did you just say that.....

Kabir - shut up! Have your seat.

Kaira - (sits with anger, whispers to Aarohi) he is khaadhos (stern) k for Kabir and k for khaadhos. Both of them giggled.

Kabir - (ended his speech) Dr. Kaira, in my cabin, right now.

CHAPTER THREE

Stranger

At times you can't admire the girl you love and end up admiring a stranger.

Aarchi Advani Saini.!

Kaira was walking through the corridor, searching for Dr. Kabir's cabin. She was suddenly hit by a guy and he was about to fall when Kaira pulled him back through his shirt.

Karan - you okay?

Kaira - I'm fine, are you okay?

Karan - yeah! I met a girl who has spider man powers. He giggled.

Kaira - oh really! Well, can you tell me where is the cabin of Dr. Khaadhos , uh, I

mean, ah, Dr. Kabir?

Karan - Bro's cabin, follow me!

Kaira - he is your brother?

Karan - yeapp, though a step one. But we love each other. Btw did you just call him khaadhos. (Stern)

Kaira - oh ! Ya ! He is khaadhos!

Karan - (laughed) girls usually find Bro hot, you are the first to call him stern. And you aren't even scared to say that.

Kaira - I don't speak about people behind their back, I'm honest with my opinions. whether it be good or bad, I say what I feel.

Karan - nice to know that. I'm Karan.

Kaira - I'm Kaira, (she smiled)

Karan - oh my! Your dimples are cute!

Kaira - hehe, thenkuuu.

Karan - you mean thank you

Kaira - it's the same

Karan - you are kiddish.

They reached the cabin. Knock knock

Kabir - come in Bro!

Karan - how do you know it's me?

Kabir - (got up to hug him) I know.

(Kaira sneaked in)

Kaira - may I come in?

Kabir - you are already in miss

Kaira - oh ya,(she stood behind Karan) Btw why did you call me Dr. Kabir.

(Before Kabir could say something, a girl in a descent black dotted dress, entered. It's Aarti ppl)

Aarti - hey! How are you, baby?

Kaira - (moved back to Karan's ear) did she just call your huge Bro, a baby?

Karan - she is her fiancee and my sister-in-law.

Kaira - oh ! I feel pity for her , marrying such a stern human.

Karan - my Bro is not that bad.

Kaira - hmm hmm

Aarti - did you have your lunch baby ?

Kabir - not yet , I'll have it soon Aaru.

Kaira - he even calls her Aaru , (giggles)

Aarti - you don't take care of yourself, you are soo..... (Her phone ranged and she went outside)

Kaira - if baby - Aaru are done can I leave.

Kabir - karan , wait outside.

Karan - ok Bro! (He whispers) all the best kairu !

Kaira - kairu??¿¿

Kabir got up from his seat and went closer to kaira,

Kabir - So Dr. Kaira, it's a hospital

Kaira - oh I thought it's shopping mall. I know that.

Kabir - oh ! you know that. I thought you forgot. Let me say you this for the first and last time that this is a hospital and you are here for your internship. Focus on that and
not on any mischievous crap.

Kaira - (yawning and snapping her fingers in front of her lips)

Kabir - (he gets angry when somebody don't pay attention to him) Dr. Kaira (he yelled)

Kaira - (present again) ya , I get it. Don't yell, I'm not deaf khaadhos. Uh Dr. Kabir.

Kabir - you may leave .

Kaira was walking to the door and kabir called her

Kabir - and ya I'm not khaadhos.

Kaira - that's what I'm gonna decide. Not you . Have a good day kabira

Kabir - Dr. Psycho! (HE smiled out of nowhere, he admired kaira's smile in his heart)

Aarti arrived and soon he realised that now he can't even admire any other girl other than Aarti.

Kaira knocked at the cabin again

Kabir was having food, actually Aarti was making him eat.

Kabir - come in.

Kaira - ya , oh sholly to disturb you
the patients file is compiled where should I keep it.

Kabir - over theeerreee (food inside his mouth) was it sorry

Kaira - ya its the same. you are such a baby , first finish what's inside your mouth.

Aarti's eyes widened at that statement.

Kabir - controlled his smile and pointed his finger at the drawer. Kaira placed the file inside and saw a picture of his when he was a kid.

Kaira - awh ! You were soo cute as a kid.

(She realised that he was with his fiancee so she went quite.) And ya , I need the forms for interns.

Kabir - that's with Mr. Khanna

Kaira - oh the complain boy !

Kabir - (started laughing) ya. Why complain boy

Kaira - I swear he is soo tall , my neck aches when I talk to him.

Aarti was annoyed and walked away .

Kaira - Btw, your fiancee is possessive about you.

Kabir - how can you make it out.

Kaira - pretty easy, her facial expressions when you laugh at my silly jokes is a sign. Now you have your food and call your Aaru who calls you a baby.

Kabir - you! !!

Kaira left and Aarti came in.

Aarti - it seems like you really enjoy her stupid jokes.

Kabir - it's not like that Aaru, it's just that ....

To be continued.

CHAPTER FOUR

Space

It's not just girls, but at times even boys need some space.
They don't express themselves because they want to be
understood and loved before they say.
Aarchi Advani Saini.!
Kabir - it's just that she has an adorable personality, and
she is a bit notorious. (Surprised to realize that he finds
kaira cute)
Aarti - And may I know what's soo funny about her
jokes.
Kabir - they are just silly.
Aarti - is it necessary to laugh at silly
things?
Kabir - oh please Aaru, let's not argue on that.
Aarti - argue? Am I arguing with you?
Kabir - no you are not . I am sorry .
Aarti - you better be sorry.
Kabir was silent. Somewhere he is regretting that
because of their parents decision his best friend had
turned into his fiancee. And most importantly she is
possessive about him. He doesn't have his own space now.
Aarti - okay , listen I have an important meeting to
attend. So I won't be able to join you for dinner.

Kabir - but Aaru Mrs. Sinha have specially planned it for you.

Aarti - I know ! But meeting is important Kabir.

Kabir - fine ! Attend your meetings.

Aarti - oh my baby , I'm sorry , I'll surely make it next time. Bye.

Aarti leaves his cabin. Kabir is left alone with his thoughts. He was busy thinking about Aarti and a sudden flash of kaira's face falls in front of his eyes.

Kabir - ah ! Why am I dreaming about her. What's wrong g with you kabir, are you in upar senses, control yourself. She is just a psycho.

Kaira knocks at his cabin and came in

Kaira - kabiraa I need your signature here.

Kabir - why are you in my dreams kaira?

Kaira - (moves closer to kabir and sits on his table. She pulls his cheeks) Dr. Kabir you are not dreaming.

Kabir - (realises that she is here) oh , sorry.

Kaira - (goes back to where she was standing and calls kabir.)

Kabir - (still lost and smiling)

Kaira - I think I should come closer to you again to bring you back to the reality.

Kabir - oh ! Sorry !

Kaira - is it sorry day today. Stop apologizing for it.

Kabir - you didn't mind the fact that I wasn't attentive.

Kaira - nooohh kabiraa , why would I? Sign here.

Kabir - (signs the document) Dr. Psycho can I ask you something?

Kaira - sure kabira , go ahead.

Kabir - I know it's a bit personal but have you ever been in love.

Kaira - (felt her Heartache for she recollected the past) ah , no ! (Without making an eye contact)

Kabir - Dr. Psycho do you know that you can't lie.

Kaira - how do you know that I was lying.

Kabir - because when you lie you don't make an eye contact. Am I right ?

Kaira - when did you notice that.

Kabir - today morning when you lied to Mr. Khanna , oh I mean the complain boy when he asked you about are you free this evening.

Kaira - oh! I swear I get a feeling that this complain boy has gone mad.

Kabir - (laughs) you made him so.

Kaira - me ? What did I do ? Even Dr. Witch says the same.

Kabir - Dr. Witch ??

Kaira - yes oh , I mean Dr. Ritu

Kabir - you named her Witch!

Kaira - yeapp, though she is pretty good but her nails are kinda long and I hate people who maintains long nails.

Kabir - (places his hand behind the desk and looks at his nails) they are fine.

Kaira - kabiraa, your nails doesn't matter .

Kabir - why so ?

Kaira - because that's my hate factor for girls and for boys , it's their hair.

Kabir - oh! Mine are kinda long.

Kaira - no , they aren't! Your messy hairs look cute!

Kabir - (smiled as the word cute echoed in his heart)

Kaira - okie , I'll leave, (she turned facing her back , while the files on Kabir's table fell on the ground) oii Sholly!

Kabir - it's OK! Calm down ! You mean sorry ?

Kaira - it's the same kabira !

Kabir - why do you keep giving names to people around you.

Kaira - I love giving nick names to people I love

Kabir - you love ?

Kaira - ya I love !

Kabir - So you love me ?

Kaira - ah ! No ! I mean ......

To be continued......

CHAPTER FIVE

Broken Side

No matter how annoying and talkative a person can be they always have that one deep and broken side of theirs which they don't show as they are scared.

Aarchi Advani Saini.!

Kaira - oh! No ! I mean. . . . .uh ! I like you as a doctor.

Kabir - hmm.... I see!

Kaira - ya , you see , so now can I go out of your sight. I have a patient to attend.

Kabir - (giggles) sure !

(Kaira noticed his dimples)

Kaira - wait ! Do you get dimples like me ?

Kabir - yeah ! They are tiny.

Kaira - awh ! They are cute.

Kabir - why do use "awh" all the time.

Kaira - can't help it !

(Kaira gets up and leaves. Kabir had a very important surgery to attend and other doctors are gonna attend him. The rest of the doctors were at lunch and there was no one when an accident case arrived. Kaira was walking towards her cabin when she saw him. He was her past lying on a stretcher, bleeding from head. She rushed towards him , ignoring the flashes of her bad past.)

Kaira - Adi ! Adi ! (Taps his cheeks)

(she asks the doctors on lunch to attend him but they refused saying if they don't eat they can't work. Kaira was pissed and entered the another operation theater herself. She took some cotton to wipe his

blood and then took a needle to stitch his wounds. Though she could heal his scars but couldn't heal her own given by him. She can't see much of blood and was feeling unconscious but she was determined to heal him. Kabir was done with his surgery and came looking for her as she had a meeting to attend.)

Kabir - (stops a nurse midway) Nurse, where's Dr . Kaira?

Nurse - she is attending an accident patient Dr. Kabir.

Kabir - what ! Where is she ?

Nurse - in the O.T

(Kabir rushes towards the O.T ,his blood was boiling as no doctor without experience is supposed to attend a critical case , he opens the door and looks at kaira. Her eyes filled with tears , her fingers trembling to place to bandage and her face so pale)

Kabir - Dr. Kaira your okay? Let me handle this. (His anger was flushed away as he saw her)

Kaira - kabir , just see him , he is bleeding a lot........ah..... there were no doctors ... so....so I did it myself.

Kabir - it's okay , leave it for me , I'll do it .

Kaira - hmm. (Wipes her tears and leaves. She rushes towards her cabin and shuts the door. Crying) why? Why it's me all the time. I just asked that i don't want to see him but I never said that in this situation. It's all his fault, I know. I remember saying him to drive safely but he never listened to me ! Now who is suffering!?

(Kabir does the observation and was quite impressed with the fact that no matter how annoying Dr. Kaira is she is good to her work. He came out and then went to his cabin. He took of his diary.)

~ I have always seen her annoying people,

but today when I saw her crying I just had an urge in my heart to wipe her tears. I don't know why I can't hate her but I can't love her either.~

Kabir walks towards kaira's cabin.

knocks at the door

Kaira - (Wipes her tears)come in

Kabir - You okay Dr. Kaira?

Kaira - oh it's you kabira, I'm fine.

Kabir - you know him ?

Kaira - no ! I don't know him.

Kabir - (knew that she was lying. But he preferred to be quite at this. Someone taps his shoulder from the back. A young girl dressed in blue with hairs falling on her face and teary eyes.)

Girl - excuse me, huh , can you tell me where is Aditya , he just met with an accident.

Kabir - oh ! He is in room 206 , he is fine now.

Kaira - (looks at the girl) Rohi ! Go and meet him , he needs you !

Rohi - Kaira! Ah , okay!

(Rohi leaves and kabir is silent, thinking of all the possible relations these three can have.)

Kaira - he is my ex -boyfriend and she is his current girlfriend.

Kabir - (shocked) but why did you say that to me .

Kaira - oh kabiraa, don't pressurise your little brain, I knew what we're you thinking.(smiles)

Kabir - (smiles and nodded) we have a meeting a now to attend. Come to the conference room.

Kaira - (walked along with kabir , hands in the pocket of her white court and humming)

Kabir - can you be quite for a while ?!!??

Kaira - Khaadhos mood activated.

Kabir - *stares* what did you say?

Kaira - oh! Nothing! Not intense looks Pleashhhh, they are scary.

Kabir - please**

Kaira - pleeaasshhhh !

Kabir - forget it !

(Reaches the conference room and nobody arrived yet. Kaira was touching the walls and humming again)

Kabir - didn't I ask you to be quite?

Kaira - (ignores him)

Kabir - (walks towards her , corners her towards the wall and stands facing her closely) what kind of human are you, your ex just met with an accident, you were crying a moment ago and now you are humming!!

Kaira - uh , uh , kabiraa aren't you too close to ask this......

To be continued.......

CHAPTER SIX

Hate

At times it's hard to hate that one person whom you once loved madly neither you can trust him as you use to nor you bear his presence.

Aarchi Advani Saini.!

Kabir - answer me first dammit!

Kaira - ssshhh!! Don't yell at me! (She pushes kabir behind, pulls him by his hand and corners him to the wall) What do you think of yourself, I don't owe you anything and stop yelling at me ! Don't you dare control me get it ! And ya I'm Sholly because I attended the patient. There were no doctors available. They were busy with their lunch. Oh ! Thenkuuu for reminding, I gotta deal with them

Kabir - hmm !

Kaira - good! (Moves back)

Kabir - what are you gonna do now?

Kaira - (evil laugh) haha just wait and watch

Kabir - Dr. Psycho please don't do any kind of....

Kaira - ssshhh ! Let me plan what should I do

Kabir - such a devil you are

Kaira - a aaann , devil's mom *smirking*

Kabir - whatever .

(Everybody entered the conference room and the meeting began. All the ideas were discussed and renovation was decided. Everybody started leaving the room and their was Mrs. Sinha asking kabir how is he)

Kaira - Mrs. Sinha

Mrs. Sinha - yes Dr. Kaira

Kaira - ma'am I have an opinion about my cabin.

Mrs. Sinha - sure Dr. Kaira go ahead

Kaira - can my cabin be painted in pink ?

Mrs. Sinha - umm , Pink ?¿

Kabir - The colours are decided it's blue and white.

Kaira - im not talking to you khaadhos, I'm talking to your mom , now ssshh.

Mrs. Sinha - (looks at kabir them kaira and giggles) ah , sure dear

Kaira - oh! Thenkuuu shoo much maam! (She leans forward and hugs her)

Kabir - (starring at her) It's thank you Dr. Kaira

Kaira - it's the same kabira, and your mom is really sweet.

Mrs. Sinha - it's OK

(Kaira is about to leave and then turns back to give a flying kiss to Mrs. Sinha. In
a flow she keeps her fingers on her lips and was about to direct it towards kabir)

Kaira - umm , u don't need it , anyways tata , have a good day ma'am and you too khaadhos.

(She leaves)

Mrs. Sinha - (giggles) when did she join

Kabir - she is an intern here and interns don't have a cabin

Mrs. Sinha - oh! No problem let her work here after she is done with her studies. It will be her cabin. Let me spoil her a bit. I love girls like her. I wish even Aarti has a bit of her.

Kabir - as you wish , she is spoiled already Mrs. Sinha. And Aarti is fine the way she is. And this Dr. Psycho is unbearable.

Mrs. Sinha - you will surely change your statement one day as you get to know her son.

Kabir - hmm

———————

Aarohi - kaira are you fine

Kaira - yeapp, absolutely fine

Aarohi - at least don't lie to me

Kaira - (turns back and hugs her) you know my heart was pounding when I saw Adi in that situation.

Aarohi - do you still love him

Kaira - no I don't! It's just that I can't hate him. It's hard to hate a person whom you once loved madly.

Aarohi - I can understand. You'll soon find someone who loves you madly.

Kaira - hope so , (Her voice was heavy as her heart was falling apart.) I don't even feel like there is someone who loves me.

Aarohi - aahhhh! Stop it kaira, people love you stupid.

Kaira - I don't think so. When I love people all I get back is pain.

Aarohi - pain for time being. There is surely someone who will find his way to you.

(Kabir was about to knock but he heard kaira weeping , so he slightly opened the door to see her. He saw her hugging Aarohi and weeping. Cheeks all red and eyes are drenched.)

Kaira - does kabir eats marshmallows?

Aarohi - yeah ! Why are you asking this all of a sudden
?
Kaira - umm , nothing .....
Aarohi - you can't hide it my dimple queen! Now spill it
out.
Kaira - his mouth smells like marshmallows.
Aarohi - oh ! How do you know , did he kiss you?
Ahaan ahann
Kaira - no dumbhead, of course not. He just ....
To be continued.........

CHAPTER SEVEN

Winning hearts

Girls are the way too good at two things:
1. Winning hearts and,
2. Winning arguments.
Don't mess with them either you will lose the battle or give away your heart.

Aarchi Advani Saini.!

Kaira - he just got so close to me and his mouth smelled like marshmallows *blushes and scratches her head*

Aarohi - *laughs* ohh , but why?

Kaira - oh! Because I was humming and he didn't like it. Or maybe it was something else.

Aarohi - umm, what something?

Kaira - can't guess.

(Karan comes in her cabin and greets her)

Karan - hi spider woman

Karan - oh it's you ! Hi karan

(Aarohi is blank)

Karan - kairu , whose she ? (He smiles at Aarohi)

Aarohi - I'm her best friend

Karan - ah ! I see

Kaira - oh yes ! Karan I need your help. Will you

Karan - sure kairu , anything for you.

Kairu - firstly stop calling me kairu, pleasshhh, and next I have a plan *evil laugh*

Karan - what plan

Aarohi - baby noo you aren't doing anything.

Kaira - chill Aaru baby , everything will be fine.

Karan - *coughs* baby ??

Kaira - hehe , (side hugs Aarohi and kisses on her cheeks) she is my Aaru baby.

Aarohi - and she's mine , before anyone

else's

Karan - the most cringy besties I've ever seen.

(Discusses the plan)

Karan - no wonder Kaira , you just look innocent and cute but ......

Kaira - huh ! I know karan , I'm a devil *makes her eyebrows dance*

Aarohi - baby , do you think it's fine ?

Kaira - of course my Aaru baby, just wait and watch. They neglected an accident case , they have to pay for it !

(At night , Kabir was staring at the stars , he doesn't appears to be but he is a poetic person.)

Kabir - no wonder these stars tell me something I don't know and the moon smiles at me. I wish I could love people the way they loved me. I miss you mum. (Warm tears started rolling down his cheeks and he wiped them immediately)

The next morning -

Kaira - come on kaira, you can do it , show that stupid doctor what had he done and make him regret his mistakes. (She reaches the hospital and karan and Aarohi are having a conversation)

Karan - so Aarohi , how long it's been that you know kairu

Aarohi - didn't she ask you not to address her as kairu! Umm it's been 20 yrs

Karan - oh ya ! Woahhhh! Really , that's a bit more

Aarohi - yep , we know each other since our childhood.

Karan - I see, boy friend

Aarohi - isn't that too personal karan.

Karan - I'm asking about Kaira's

Aarohi - I'm saying this only for her. You needn't need to know that.

Karan - (rubs the back of his neck and

glares at Aarohi. Her deep brown eyes and her dark eyebrows, her tiny nose and her rosy lips) you are pretty

Aarohi - thanks , and stop staring me .

(Kaira enters)

Kaira - all set? ?

Karan - yeapp

Aarohi - I'll just get the rope (she leaves)

Karan - your Aaru baby is pretty

Kaira - you forgot me soo soon , so pathetic,

Karan - (places his hand on her shoulder) not really my kairu

Kaira - ssshhh ! Get lost !

———————————

(Kabir was discussing the process of a surgery with his senior doctors)

Kabir - So I think open heart surgery is necessary, there's no other option.

Kaira - (knocks at the door and comes inside) kabiraa I need your help.

Kabir - I'm busy at least wait till I say come in.

Kaira - I don't have much time khaadhos, you are helping me or not ?

Kabir - no ! I'm busy

Kaira - expected, I hate you !

Kabir - (eye rolls) I hate you to

Kaira - I hate you three

Kabir - I hate you ten (raises his eyebrows)

Kaira - (smirks) I hate you infinity. There's no number which comes after infinity! I won !

Kabir - do you love winning arguments or what !!??

Kaira - huh ! I'm way too good at two things - winning hearts and winning arguments. (Flips her not-so-long hair)

Kabir - whatever

Kaira - (grinds her teeth) ugh ! Khaadhos!

(She leaves the cabin and goes to the pharmacy)

Kaira - give me some anesthesia

Pharamacist - here (handles her the bottle)

Kaira - thenkuuu

(She leaves and goes the O.T , karan and Aarohi were waiting there for her)

Kaira - Sholly ppl , soo how is it going

Karan - ya......

To be continued..........

CHAPTER EIGHT

Incomplete

Love can never happen at first sight. It's just attraction. Love can't disappear but just leaves something incomplete.

Aarchi Advani Saini.!

Karan - yeapp! Waiting for your orders my majesty

Aarohi - (giggles) Karan, stop it

Karan - (whispers to kaira) your bestie kills me with her smile , hayeee , I'm dead

Kaira - should a book a grave?

Aarohi - for ?

Kaira - karan

Karan - aaee , shut up ! I was .... I was kidding

Kaira - you can't even die for my bestie , you are a bad spot on the love story of romeo juliet , heer-raanjha, etc etc

Karan - I can kaira , but I wanna live with her and die with her.

Kaira - I don't know how you guys get soo serious about a girl within seconds, I mean, really ?

Karan - love at first sight you see

Kaira - the only law of psychology that I disagree with is " it takes you seven seconds to fall in love"

Karan - really ! But I just took three , so even i disagree with it .

Kaira - huh ! Just Ssshhh! Now you both listen , Dr. Ajay is attending a patient right now and as soon as he leaves his cabin you Aaru, go and talk to him friendly and bring him to the O.T here. Meanwhile you karan , you'll help me with catching him. Ok

Karan - ya okay , but will Aaru be safe

Aarohi - (blinks her eyes at karan) umm....ah....

Kaira - Aarohi! It's Aarohi. And of course she is. My baby Aaru knows how to protect herself.

(Aarohi leaves and meets Dr. Ajay)

Aarohi - he is in the O.T. Dr.Ajay , I just had few complications

Ajay - it's OK Aarohi. I'll help you dear!

(They reached the O.T and then bham! Karan covers his head with blanket and kaira traps him in rope.)

Ajay - leave me , Aarohi what are you doing ? You could have said me before. I would have booked a hotel room for you darling

Kaira - (really angry) you stupid duffer , (bangs his head)

Karan - you asshole! ! (Kicks his ass)

(Everybody could hear the noise and came rushing to the room)

Kabir - (opens the door and looks at kaira beating him) Dr. Psycho have you lost it . Stop it . (He holds kaira from the back)

Kaira - leave me kabiraa , I'll smack his face, I'll split his head into two parts, I swear I'll kill him , leave me kabiraa !!

Kabir - calm down Dr. Psycho (grips her tight in his arms and pulls her towards him from the back)

Kaira - I won't spare you ! You donkey, you monkey, you idiot , stupid , (she kicks Dr. Ajay's legs when kabir tries to lift her up)

Kabir - Dr. Psycho you are mad.....calm down

Kaira - you don't know kabira , he is an asshole, I'll kill him. You asking me to calm down! First fire him .

Kabir - ok calm down first

(The entire staff was shocked but all they noticed was kabir holding kaira in his arms)

Kaira - firstly, he didn't attend a critical case, he was hungry , this stupid homo sapien was hungry and next he spoke disgustingly with Aaru,

Kabir - Aarti? ?

Kaira - no ! There's not just your Aaru on this planet , I'm talking about Aarohi.

Kabir - What ? (Anger flushed over his face)

Kaira - he said that

Kabir - no need to explain Dr. Psycho! I'll deal with this (he gets closer to ajay)

Kabir - let me teach him how to behave with a girl,

(Then dishoom dishoom wala scene?)

Kabir - you are fired Dr. Ajay, get lost I'll make sure that even your licence gets cancelled.

Kaira - thenkuuu kabiraa

Kabir - it's OK Dr. Psycho!

Kaira - your lips, it's bleeding

Kabir - (Wipes it) ah , it's fine

Kaira - sure ?

Kabir - yeah!

(Not every scene can be romantic readers?)

Kabir reaches his cabin and saw Aarti sitting on the chair

Kabir - oh ! Hi Aaru

Aarti - hi ! So did I hear the truth

Kabir - about ?

Aarti - oh ! Don't pretend ! The entire staff is talking about how you hugged that kaira from behind !

Kabir - Dr. Kaira ! Address her as Dr! And I didn't hug her !

Aarti - oh really! Then what was that ?

Kabir - I was just ....

To be continued

CHAPTER NINE

Death

Losing someone whom you truly loved isn't less of death.

Aarchi Advani Saini.!

Kabir - I just pushed her back and holded her , that's it ! Holding someone isn't termed as a hug !

Aarti - whatever. Your lips, it's bleeding Kabir !

Kabir - oh ! Ya ! It's fine , I'm alright.

Aarti - no you aren't! Sit down here , let me see.

Kabir - it's OK Aaru, I'm fine

Aarti - sit ! Umm , let me place a bandage here.

Kabir - no Aaru, no need. You can't place it near my lips, it's weird.

Aarti - well , I can place something else on your lips. (She smirks and bits her lower lip)

Kabir - no need , place the bandage.

Aarti - good boy !

(Kabir wore a mask to hide his bandage. He was walking towards the conference room)

Kaira - hollaaa ! Khaadhos

Kabir - hmm

Kaira - say holaa

Kabir - (types a message on his phone and shows her) I can't talk

Kaira - why ? Did your Aaru ordered you to ?

Kabir - (turns to her and removes his mask) hmm

Kaira - (pushes her lips inside to control her laugh but indeed a vain attempt) hahaha , you look so cute khaadhos

Kabir - (stares at her , types) I knew that you will laugh , that's why I wasn't showing it .

Kaira - okie okie , Sholly

Kabir - (types) sorry**

Kaira - you can't speak but you still wanna correct me ! Khaadhos!

(They reached the conference room)

Kaira - let me remove it or else you can't discuss anything (laughs)

Kabir - hmm

(Kabir is pretty tall , so kaira was standing on her toes but still couldn't reach)

Kabir - (smiles)

Kaira - you too a complain boy (she drags a chair a stands on it. She leaned forward towards kabir and her tiny fingers reached the bandage. She placed her right hand on his cheek and slowly stated pulling out the bandage)

Kaira- ah ! Sholly , does it hurt ?

Kabir - no

(Kabir is lost , glancing kaira. Her hazel brown eyes, rosy pink lips , curly lashes and shinning cheeks. He couldn't stop himself from looking at her)

Kaira - ha , done!

Kabir - umm, thanks

Kaira - your welcome!

(Kabir sat on his chair and reads the reports)

Kaira - what is it kabiraa

Kabir - a report of a patient, his blood vessels are blocked and his heart isn't getting enough blood. We need to do a open heart surgery.

Kaira - ah ! Ah ! Open heart surgery, is it necessary?

Kabir - it is Dr. Psycho

Kaira - Huunnhh! !!!

Kabir - stop mourning like a child , you don't even know him.

Kaira - so what! I have a relationship of humanity with every human being.

Kabir - uhh!

Kaira - you are such a heartless doctor

Kabir - I'm a heart specialist, not a heartless doctor.

Kaira - you are a heartless doctor who is a heart specialist. (She went sad)

Kabir - really Dr. Psycho! You are being sad for a stranger.

Kaira - hmm. How can you just pierce his skin and murder his chest .

Kabir - it's is 6 open heart surgery, so relax.

Kaira - oh my goodness, you assassinated 6 hearts

Kabir - assassinated ??¿¿

Kaira - ya ! Haven't you lost any patient

Kabir - nope.

Kaira - that's painful

Kabir - what ? Not losing any patient ?

Kaira - no khaadhos, the surgery.

Kabir - it's hard to lose someone you love. Did you lose anyone in your life ?

Kaira - hmm , my dad !

Kabir - oh ! I'm sorry

Kaira - you needn't need to be. You didn't kill him though.

Kabir - I was Aditya's name

Kaira - he was never mine to lose

Kabir - how old were you when your dad passed away?

Kaira - I was 10

Kabir - even i was 10 , we were the same age

Kaira - no kabira ,

Kabir - why no ! You were 10 and even i was 10

Kaira - oh my dear kabiraa , you are 29 now and I'm 24 , we have a difference of 5 years. So when I was 10 , you were 15 and when you were 10 , I was 5 yr old . Get it

Kabir - oh ! Ya ! *scratches his head*

Kaira - (giggles) I often think you have a split personality disorder

Kabir - (laughs) why so ?

Kaira - don't you think so , I mean , at times you are soo cute , you laugh , you smile and you talk to me and at times you are ignorant and such a khaadhos!

Kabir - ok now leave. I have to plan the surgery.

Kaira - see , now you have become khaadhos!

Kabir - Dr. Psycho if you won't leave, I'll eventually press my lips against yours

Kaira - ah aah na na , I'm going tata I won't let you kiss me

Kabir - really. ..... let's see......

To be continued. ....

CHAPTER TEN

Stingy

Loving someone shouldn't be based on genders making each other feel special makes us happy so don't be stingy. Aarchi Advani Saini.!

Kabir - really ! Let's see then (he gets up from his chair)

Kaira - ah.. ah..kabiraa, stop. I'm going tata .....(She closes the door and breathes with relief) Huhhhh! !

Kabir - such a psycho! (HE laughs)

It's been two weeks, and all interns are prepared to assist patients. These days Kabir and Kaira had a good time. Though she keeps irritating him but he was fine with that. Kaira is an intern psychologist so she will be counselling people. The way she deals with her patients is pretty impressive as she talks to them like she knows them for a long time. Kabir was done with his and was on rounds, and observing every intern. He comes across Kaira's session room. He opened the door a bit to listen.

Kaira - and it's okay to express what you feel , it's just a myth that men don't cry.

Patient - Dr. Kaira it's easy to say , but I hardly trust people around me.

Kaira - you don't need anyone by your side buddy ! I know it feels lonely , but you are only person who will never betraye yourself in the world full of demons.

Patient - Men are expected to be strong and I am. But I fall weak sometimes. And after a heart break , I'm just dead.

Kaira - hmm, I see ! Do you hate her.

Patient - I can't hate her Dr.

Kaira - so do you still feel for her ?

Patient - yes , I just want her back in my life.

Kaira - have you spoken to her ?

Patient - no ! But I want to

Kaira - then what are you waiting for . Go ahead, talk to her . Solve the matter , and I'm sure she will understand.

Patient - do you think so

Kaira - of course , just make sure to not raise your voice and don't get angry. Just hold her in your arms and whispere I love you. At times that's all a girl needs.

Patient - thank you so much Dr.

Kaira - my pleasure.

(Kaira opens her drawer and lifts up an envelope, navy blue in colour with a daisy in the centre.

Kabir closes the door and walks to the other room.

Kaira comes out of the cabin and sneaks in kabir's cabin. Places the envelope on his table. And leaves.)

Kabir - Aaru, pick up my phone !! This girl never receives my call ! (He notices the envelope)

Kabir - (reads out himself) HAPPY MENS DAY !

Kaira - woahhhh! You read it ! (She smiled adorably)

Kabir - yeah ! But this wasn't needed!

Kaira - I know you guys pretty well , even if you ppl need some special attention and treatment, you won't ask for it , unlike girls !

Kabir - we are not emotional like you ppl.

Kaira - na , you are. You do have emotions but just that you are scared to express.

Kabir - we live in a society of Myths!

Kaira - I know that pretty well kabira , but the matter of fact is do you believe those Myths !?

Kabir - maybe yes maybe no

Kaira - giving you this envelope, just had one intention and that's to make you feel special.

Kabir - and why do you wanna make me feel special

Kaira - because you deserve to feel special. When girls on their periods, they get a special treatment , from family or from their partner. But things aren't such in your case and even you ppl need some sort of it.

Kabir - hmm . But nobody understands this.

Kaira - true , I agree ! You ppl are strong !
You ppl hide a lot. You don't expect much but want to be loved. You ppl don't demand things all you need is just a little care.

Kabir - true. We don't cry as it signifies weakness, and we are known to be strong. We don't get emotional as we expected to be practical minded. We do care for ones we love but they end up taking it as possessiveness or insecurity!

Kaira - possessiveness is love and insecurity is absence of love.

Kabir - what do you mean ?

Kaira - see , when a person is possessive about you, it means he/she truly loves you and is protective about you. Insecurities arise when there is absence of love and trust in a relationship. You doubt , you face insecurity only when you don't trust !

Kabir - but girls don't like possessiveness!

Kaira - yeah ! Some don't or many don't but
I like guys who are possessive!
Kabir - really?
Kaira - of course , when they have that she's my girl
type attitude, hayeee, I lobe it!
Kabir - I swear your husband is the........

To be continued. ....

CHAPTER ELEVEN

Trust

Love is a feeling you need to feel. But before feeling the feeling you need to believe it and place your trust in it.

Aarchi Advani Saini.!

Kabir - really! Your husband is the luckiest man ! I envy him now!

Kaira - indeed he is ! But he is taking so long . *frowns*

Kabir - (giggles) he don't want to get tortured by you

Kaira - really kabira ! *sniffs*

Kaira - (laughs out loud)

Kaira - you are soo mean , I hate you

Kabir - I hate you too ! But thanks for the envelope and conversation.

Kaira - uuhhh! Did my ears just hear that ! Seriously! I can't believe this!

Kabir - So called "dramatic psycho "

Kaira - pleasures all mine. And it's not a particular day that you need to celebrate a Mens day or Women's day ! But just make each other feel special about their presence.

Kabir - hmm. I'm seeing a girl for the first time taking a guys side.

Kaira - really !

Kabir - yeah ! And girls like you are rare .

Kaira - umm not rare , they don't exist. I'm just one! A masterpiece you see !

Kabir - you started again , (Taps his palm on his forehead) *bham !!

Kaira - hehe , that was hard

Kabir - ah ! Rubs his forehead!

(Both were laughing)

Kabir - but I still hate you

Kaira - ugh! I'll ask Aarti to torture you

Kabir - she's doing it enough (he realises that he is being friendly towards kaira but he wasn't sure so he went quite)

Kaira - now I'll spread the word !*makes her eyebrows dance*

Kabir - no ! Don't! Dr. Psycho you are not doing it

Kaira - I will kabira ,

Kabir - I won't spare you !

(Kaira leaves his room and Aarti enters)

Aarti - wait what was she doing here ?

Kabir - hi ! (Tries to ignore)

Aarti - hi ! What was she doing here ?

Kabir - nothing just came to drop few files.

Aarti - oh !

Kabir - arey ya , Aaru, do you know it's Mens day today!

Aarti - really ! Happy mens day baby! *giggles*

Kabir - thanks (a bit disappointed)

Aarti - (giggles) I mean , really? Why do men need it !

Kabir - why don't we need it !

Aarti - like I mean , *laughs* what will you ppl do. Wish each other a 'HAPPY MENS DAY' !really

Kabir - no but just make each other feel special.

Aarti - oh ! But isn't it awkward , like. Girls treating boys in a special way ,

Kabir - why awkward? Isn't it awkward when is vice versa

Aarti - not really instead it's cute and obligatory !

Kabir - obligatory? ?

Aarti - yes , of course! Anyways kabir I have an important interview, so I'm going to London for a week. Ok , I'll be back soon.

Kabir - hmm.

(Kaira was walking towards her cabin and met karan)

Kaira - oh ! Holaa

Karan - holaa , wassup

Kaira - I'm great ! How are you?

Karan - well I'm charming and handsome!

Kaira - ugh ! Disgusting, hi Aaru !

Karan - hi *surprised*

Kaira - hehe , look at you

Karan - Kairaaaa , you scared me man

Kaira - Sholly, (she was a bit serious)

Karan - oh my ! I've never seen you so serious, what happened?

Kaira - nothing

Karan - common on kaira , you can share

Kaira - you know I always thought it's just me who is scared to love but even kabiraa is

Karan - no ! He is getting married man

Kaira - no karan , he never loved Aarti. And he is scared to love and trust people, after his mums death , he doesn't believe in love anymore.

Karan - that's true ! Bro's mum passed away when he was a kid and my dad left me and my mum at the same time. Mummy and dad , uh , that is my mum and Bro's dad were childhood friends, so their families got them married.

I accepted dad as my father because I was just five bit Bro loved his mum a lot and couldn't accept the replacement.

Kaira - ohh , I see ! But I really want kabira to accept Mrs. Sinha as his mum.

Karan - even i want to but I can't.

Kaira - I will ! Kabira can't live his entire life without loving and accepting ppl. And when Mrs. Sinha loves him so much then what's pulling him back ? I'll make him trust over love again.

Karan - Kaira!

Kaira - hmm

Karan - thanks for being here

Kaira - oh karan , don't be so formal. It's my job anyways. I make ppl believe in themselves and love to.

Karan - I know ! But what's weird is Aarti never tried to bring Bro and mum closer , though she is going to be the daughter in law of the Sinha family. She doesn't care .

Kaira - oh ! I'll do something like. .....

CHAPTER TWELVE

Personalities

Weird personalities make different love stories.
Aarchi Advani Saini.!
Kaira - I'll do something for sure!
Karan - and you know right, if you need any help I'm always there.
Kaira - of course, I know that. Hi Aaru baby
Karan - oh! You can't fool me this time, I know she isn't here.
Kaira - *giggles* really! Ok tell me how she looks
Karan - ah! I wish I could describe her through words but she is a goddess, and I'm a human who is making vain attempts
to weave her into words.
Kaira - oh my! What a line
Karan - ah! When she smiles, it's a bullet that pierces my heart,
Kaira - ahann , what else
Karan - and her eyes, hayee, they are twinkling stars, and her cheeks
(Aarohi taps his shoulder)
Aarohi - done, or anything left
Karan - oh. .... ah...a ....Aaru. ...I. ...was....just. ...woh..... I have to meet Bro! I'll go

Kaira - bubyeee karan , tata
(Karan walks away)
Kaira - well I can see someone is blushing, oii hoii
Aarohi - kaiiraa, stop it .
Kaira - ahann ahann pink cheeks, lips curling into a
smile
Aarohi - ugh! Stop it, man, *covers her face*
Kaira - he is a nice guy. You can count on him, I believe.
Aarohi - ok now tell me how was your day going
Kaira - umm, it was nice, but now I was planning
something.
Aarohi - now whom do you wanna fight with.
Kaira - eehh, I don't always fight around with ppl..... I
just react. That's it.
Aarohi - oh really! I know you pretty well
Kaira - I know that. I was thinking about kabira.
Aarohi - ohhh, why so?
Kaira - I wanna bring him and Mrs. Sinha closer.
Aarohi - hmm. I'll help you, baby.
Kaira - thenkuuu my baby.
(The hospital hours are over. Kaira and Aarohi were
leaving and Karan came)
Karan - hola ppl
Kaira - hola, I'm leaving in a hurry, you ppl carry.
winks Aarohi
Aarohi - bye take care Kaira
Karan - bye spider woman
Kaira - tata bubyeee
(Karan and Aarohi are walking down the street. They
noticed Kaira and Kabir standing together and follow
them. Kaira was wearing a dainty embroidered dress with
a Pashmina scarf)
Kaira - hola khadhoos

Kabir - hi Dr. Psycho
Kaira - you should reply a holaa with a holaa not hi
Kabir - whatever.
Kaira - tata I'm going bubyeee.
Kabir - how are you going?
Kaira - I'm gonna walk.
Kabir - it's too late. It won't be safe.
Kaira - donno worry kabiraa, I can protect myself,
(crosses her hands) I know karate,
haaaee hahaha
Kabir - it's not safe for the guy who will get trapped by
you. I'm worried about him not you.
Kaira - uuhhh! Khaadhos khaadhos khaadhos!
Kabir - common let's walk
Kaira - hmmm (she was walking around dragging her
feet and moving her hands momentarily)
Kabir - can't you walk properly
Kaira - don't teach me.
Kabir - you are walking like a drunk man.
Kaira - whatever
Kabir - if you don't walk properly I'll lift you up in my
arms and drop you home.
Kaira- aahhhh! No need .... I will. ....walk....properly.
Kabir - good!
Kaira - why do you get soo romantic at times.
Kaira - because I know that you hate ppl who are
romantic.
Kaira - ya! I do hate them, but I still hate you
irrespective of the quality.
Kabir - you better hate me. (Kabir is shivering with
cold)
Kaira - hehe, why do wear such light shirts, can't you
wear a jacket. (She takes off her scarf and puts it around

Kabir's shoulder)
Kabir - umm, I'm fine
Kaira - I know you are not. Carry it. You look cute.
(Karan and Aarohi are following them and whispered)
Karan - ah! That's cute
Aarohi - I know right, they both look really cute together, but they don't accept that fact.
Karan - it usually happens like a guy gives his jacket to the girl, but in this case, it's contradictory.
Aarohi - ya, weird personalities make different love stories.
Karan - hmm. I agree. *smiles at Aarohi*
Aarohi - *smiles back*
Karan - Mann, your smile is killing me. *covers his face*
Aarohi - heheh , karan stop it
Karan - *blushes* (he reaches to hold Aarohi's hand)
Aarohi - *blushes* (grips his fingers)
Karan - this seems like heaven. Walking a lonely Street, with you beside me
Aarohi - I know right, indeed it is. You are feeling like heaven coz you are walking with a goddess.
Karan - ugh! You heard it ?..
To be continued ....

CHAPTER THIRTEEN

Memories

While living with people who always stay I feel for
strangers with lovely memories.
Aarchi Advani Saini.!
Aarohi - yeap! And it made my day. (She leans on
Karan's shoulder)
Karan - I'm glad I made your day.
Aarohi - will you be always by my side.
Karan - I will! But I won't promise. I'll show it to you.
Promises are made to prove. And I express.
Aarohi - damn.
Karan - look at Bro! Wearing Kaira's scarf
Aarohi - hehe , don't you think Dr. Kabir
looks good with Kaira
Karan - indeed, I do. Aarti is ..... not the right person for
Bro!
Aarohi - hmm
(They both look at each other)
Karan - are you thinking the same?
Aarohi - yaaaa!

Kabir - ok we reached
Kaira - yeap, tata khaadhos!
Good night

Kabir - good night, go inside
Kaira - I'm already here. I can go in
Kabir - I'll wait for you to go in. Common go
Kaira - I'm not a kid kabiraa
Kabir - really! (Looks at her from tip to toe) I don't think so.
Kaira - what do you mean
Kabir - you've just grown a bit taller, that's it! You are still a kid.
Kaira - I'm not. I'm a grown-up girl.
Kabir - assure this to your mum, not me.
Kaira - tata ,
Kabir - ta...... bye .
Kaira - *winks at Kabir* did you just say.....
Kabir - *smiles* go in or else...
Kaira - na na , I'm. .... going. ...tata.

The next day Mrs. Sinha came to meet Kabir.
Kabir - good morning Mrs. Sinha
Sinha - good morning beta
Kabir - do you need anything, like coffee or tea
Mrs. Sinha - no son, I'm fine.
(Kaira knocked at the door)
Kaira - may I come in?
Kabir - yes Dr. Psycho. .....umm. ..yes Dr. Kaira comes in.
Kaira - Kabiraa, Dr. Twitch is looking for you
Kabir - Dr. Twitch ??¿¿
Kaira - wait oh... Dr. Varun
Kabir - now why does he is twitch?
Kaira - haven't you noticed the way he blinks his eyes when he is nervous
Kabir - (laughs) really Dr. Psycho! You are insane.

Kaira - go ahead. He is looking for you.
(Kabir leaves and Mrs. Sinha looked at Kaira)
Kaira - Good morning Mrs. Sinha
Mrs. Sinha - Good morning dear. How are you?
Kaira - I'm cute and gorgeous as always. Hehe
Mrs. Sinha - indeed naughty girl
Kaira - I wanted to talk to you about kabira, if you don't take it personally, can I say?
Mrs. Sinha - of course, Kaira, go on I'm listening to you.
Kaira - do you love Kabir?
Mrs. Sinha - of course, I do dear. Though he doesn't like me, I love him as my eldest son.
(Kaira noticed Kabir was walking towards the cabin)
Kaira - Mrs. Sinha now I will be saying something which is bad but Pleashhhh, just cooperate with me. I need your help.
Mrs. Sinha - ok dear.
(Kabir opens the door a bit but was curious to know the conversation between Mrs. Sinha and Kaira. So he was listening to it all staying outside)
Kaira - oh really Mrs. Sinha how can you love someone like Kabir
Mrs. Sinha - Kaira you don't know him, dear, he is the best son any mother can have.
Kaira - maybe the worst one. He is so stubborn and stern.
Mrs. Sinha - he had become so. He wasn't such a boy when he was a kid. Or maybe because he thinks that I replaced his
beautiful mum, he can't accept me.
Kaira - he is always unsatisfied. Though knowing how much you love him he is still ungrateful.
Mrs. Sinha - Kaira! Stop it !

(Kabir is shocked to see that Kaira was talking negatively about him, though she appears to be annoying she was never this. And he was under guilt as he took Mrs. Sinha for granted)

Kaira - no! Mrs. Sinha, you should not love him. He doesn't value it. I'm telling you.

(Kabir was pissed off and walks away. Kaira saw the door closing)

Kaira - I'm really shoolyyy Mrs. Sinha for talking to you like that. I didn't mean it.

Mrs. Sinha - it's OK dear, I didn't mind, but you knew that Kabir was here so why didn't you stop talking about it.

Kaira - I wanted him to hear this.

Mrs. Sinha - why beta, you know the fact that he hates ppl who talk behind his back

Kaira - I know Mrs. Sinha but I'm here just for a week more and then we will never meet. So doesn't matter if I'm in his good books or not. What matters is what change I've bought in his life. And that change is acceptance of love and valuing ppl.

(Tears started rolling down Mrs. Sinha's cheeks and she hugged Kaira)

To be continued ....

CHAPTER FOURTEEN

Love

If a person is sweet towards you it doesn't mean he/she loves you. Sweetness is just a gesture often shown to strangers. Don't take it as love.
Aarchi Advani Saini.!
Mrs. Sinha - oh my God bless you with lots of happiness and love.
Kaira - thenkuuu Mrs. Sinha. It means a lot.
(Kabir walked in)
Kaira - take care of Mrs. Sinha
Kabir - Dr. Psycho! Leave my cabin.
Kaira - oh! Ya! I'm leaving.
(Kabir walks towards her and holds her hand)
Kabir - Dr. Kaira, I never thought that you can be so toxic. I know that you are annoying but.....
Kaira - oh! Kabir, stop it. You are hurting me.
Kabir - you don't know what hurt is Dr. Kaira, now I get it why your ex left you.
Kaira - kabir stop it
Kabir - get out
(Kaira was hurt. Her eyes filled with tears, they rolled down her cheeks and her nose was red. She rushed towards her cabin as she didn't want anyone to see her cry. Karan saw her and went to inform Aarohi about it)

Karan - I don't know what happened but I saw her crying.
Aarohi - shit man! Must be Dr. Kabir.
Karan - I think so, coz she came out of Bro's cabin.
Aarohi - let's see
(Karan and Aarohi were walking towards Kabir's cabin and what they saw was bliss)
Karan - oh my God, am I dreaming.
Aarohi - Kaira did it! I'm proud of her.
(Kabir placed his head on Mrs. Sinha's lap like a kid)
Karan - Kaira? Man, she is an angel, she did it,
Aarohi - but why was she crying
Karan - let's go to her cabin Aaru.
Aarohi - ya! Let's go.
Karan - Kaira! May I come in
Kaira - oh come on Karan, don't be so formal. You are going to be my brother-in-law. Hehe
Aarohi - Kaira!!!! Are you okay
Kaira - what happened to me? I'm alright.
Karan - but I saw you crying
Kaira - Karan !!! Dust sneaked in my eyes.
Aarohi - are you sure you are alright.
Kaira - hmm, (she nods her head)
Aarohi - you are not. When you answer with hmmm and Ummm.....that means you are not okay.
Kaira - he just got so rude.
Karan - I think I should leave. You guys talk.
Kaira - I didn't expect Kabir to say that
Aarohi - what did he say.
Kaira - he said now I get it why your ex left you.
Aarohi - what the hell is wrong with him, how can he say that.
Kaira - (narrates her all what she did)

Aarohi - seriously Kaira, you have made him hate you
Kaira - I'm a stranger in his life. And it
doesn't matter if he hates me or loves me.
Aarohi - really Kaira?
Kaira - hmm, just leave me alone for a while Aaru
Aarohi - no I won't leave you
Kaira - please I request
Aarohi - ok. But just for now.
Kaira - ok
(Aarohi leaves her alone and walks away.)
Karan - all good
Aarohi - not really
Karan - you can share if there's something.
Aarohi - (she said what happened)
Karan - I didn't expect this from Bro! Wait her ex?
Aarohi - ya! Remember the accident case, for which
Kaira had set a trap for Dr. Ajay. The guy who met with
the accident was Aditya.
Karan - oh! She still cares about him. And don't talk
about that Dr. Ajay, he is a ......
Aarohi - ok ok, I won't.
Karan - that tall guy is Aditya?
Aarohi - yeapp! He is still here.
Karan - that's the reason Kaira don't visit the ICU
Aarohi - yeah!

———————————————

It's been 2 days and Kaira and Kabir didn't have any
conversation. Kabir visited the ICU to check the patients.
He came across Aditya's bed.
Kabir - hello Mr. ..... Aditya
Aditya - hello Dr.
Kabir - how are you doing now.
Aditya - I'm better.

Kabir - good.

Aditya - where is Kaira

Kabir - Dr. Kaira is attending to her patients. Why

Aditya - nothing just asked

Kabir - you can share.

Aditya - *smirks* I wanna talk to her, not to her new boyfriend.

Kabir - excuse me, I'm not her boyfriend!

Aditya - oh! Stop fooling me. I've seen her around you all the time. She is bloody.....

Kabir - mind your language

Aditya - see, you can't even hear something wrong about her. And you say you are not her boyfriend.

Kabir - listen, I don't have time for all your shit.

Aditya - I don't either. She is just a desperate b****

Kabir - (holds his shirt) now if you say anything about her I'm gonna smack your face. Get it!

(Kaira came up)

Kaira - Kabir stops it. Leave him

Kabir - I'll kill this bloody human. He was speaking shit about you.

Kaira - Kabir leave him I said......

To be continued ....

CHAPTER FIFTEEN

Hurt

Once a person is hurt he/she will never make an attempt to hurt others as they can sympathize and empathize as well.

Aarchi Advani Saini.!

Kaira - Kabir leave him I said

Aditya - you moved on so easily Kaira, and you blamed me for doing the same.

Kaira - really adi, really. I was never a desperate person it's just that I love helping ppl. That's my job. And I still didn't move on. Kabir is my colleague and my mentor.

Aditya - really! Why do you help ppl when you don't know them.

Kaira - you won't understand this Aditya, coz you are emotionless.

Aditya - as if you are full of emotions.

Kaira - I don't wanna waste my time over you I've wasted it enough. And I don't owe you many explanations. So don't you dare ask me for any of it?

Aditya - I never saw this version of yours. You've changed

Kaira - you saw it all, you just ignored it and took it for granted.

(Kaira walks away)

Kabir - the nurse, gets his discharge papers.

It's was late in the night. And Kabir was struggling to sleep. Every time he closed his eyes, Kaira's face flashed in front of him. He got a text from Aarti.
Aarti - it's been two days and you didn't even bother to text me.?
Kabir - I'm sorry, I was busy. How are you
Aarti - I'm dead.
Kabir - I'm sorry Aaru.
Aarti - go he'll with your sorry Kabir. I was waiting for your text all day long.
Kabir - So you should have texted. I've got a lot of work in my life. And it's not that I ignore you. I can't bear your tantrums. Instead of asking how am I you are boosting over me.
Aarti - good night.

The next day Kabir was in his cabin and Karan came in
Karan - good morning Bro!
Kabir - good morning Karan, (he gets up to hug him)
Karan - (hugged him lightly)
Kabir - you okay? You usually hug me
tight, all good?
Karan - hmm Bro! I just wanted to take your car for today, can I
Kabir - yeah! Take it .... but why?
Karan - me and Aaru, I mean Aarohi are going out for dinner so, that's why.
Kabir - oh I see. Someone's in love.
Karan - *smiles*
Kabir - hey! What happened
Karan - you've hurt her

Kabir - whom?

Karan - Kaira!

Kabir - oh okay, I don't wanna talk about it.

Karan - do you really think Bro, that she said it all about you purposefully?

Kabir - I don't know!

Karan - bro, a girl like her, who can't see her ex in pain, who have traumatized her will hurt you. The one who is already hurt terribly will ever think of hurting someone else.

Kabir - huh!

Karan - she just did it all to bring your mum closer to each other. She doesn't like it when ppl living under the same roof hate each other.

Kabir - how do you know all this.

Karan - she said me, Bro! It was all her plan Bro!

Kabir - this Dr. Psycho is a complete psycho. (rubs his forehead)

Karan - I know you didn't know it, but now as you know, apologize to her.

Kabir - I will! I have to! I said shit, I spoke crap, shit man

Karan - be early before it's too late Bro.

Kabir - can you just bring Aarohi here. ......

Karan - yeah!

(Aarohi appears and they had a discussion)

Kabir - and I'm sorry Dr. Aarohi, I didn't mean to hurt your best friend.

Aarohi - it's OK Dr. Kabir! But I think you should apologize to her.

Kabir - yeah I will.

Kabir - guys all set

Karan - bro, lilies are not available
Kabir - umm. ... then go for baby's breath and pink
roses, Dr. Psycho loves pink.
Karan - ok Bro! And what about the fairy lights?
Kabir - adjust it somewhere
Aarohi - what somewhere Dr.Kabir, Karan put it on the
pole of curtains. Dr. Kabir I must say, you are bad at
decorating.
Kabir - *scratches his head* indeed I am. Well if I want
to do it again, I'll call you for help.
Aarohi - sure! Any time.
To be continued ....

———————————————————

CHAPTER SIXTEEN

Game

Sometimes things don't go in a way you have to plant them to and here destiny plays its own game.

Aarchi Advani Saini.!

Kabir - ok all set? Everything's ready guys?

(Karan and Aarohi in a chorus)

Yes, boss !!!

Kabir - Dr. Aarohi, just ask her to come upstairs

Aarohi - sure Dr. Kabir

(Aarohi leaves)

The entire room had pink balloons, black velvet curtains with falling fairy lights, in the center, was a huge "sorry" hanging which was dipped in glitters.

(Twist readers?)

(Aarti came up before Kaira did)

Aarti - oh my God, Kabir did you do this all for me

Kabir - (shocked) uh....ah...

Aarti - awh! That's so sweet baby!

Kabir - Aaru, actually

Karan - (holds his hand) if you want to die from her hands then spill the truth.

Kabir - she is ruining my surprise, Karan!

Karan - you just wanted to apologize to Kaira, you can do it still. I know she'll understand. And anyway, it's an apology, not a date you've set for Kaira.

Kabir - hmmm

Aarti - you were saying, something baby

Kabir - no nothing Aarti

(Aarti walked towards Kabir and hugged him)

Aarti - it's ok baby, and thank you for the surprise. I didn't know you missed me so much.

Kabir - hmm. (Aarti kissed Kabir on his cheeks.) Ah... Aarti (he brings down her hands which were around his waist)

(Kaira came with Aarohi)

Kaira - what's wrong, you bought me here to see this baby Aaru getting romantic with each other.

Aarohi - no! What the hell, what is she doing here

Kaira - Aaru what are you talking about

Aarohi - my baby, your khaadhos had set this all for you.

Kaira - (Surprised) for me

Aarohi - yes baby (raises her eyebrows at Karan)

Karan - (shrugged his shoulders) hi Aaru!

Aarti - no Karan, only Kabir can call me that

Karan - I addressed Aarohi as Aaru, not you Aarti

(Aarti turned around and saw Kaira and Aarohi)

Aarti - hi both of you

Kaira - hi!

Aarti - hi to you to the lady (she waved her hands at Aarohi)

Aarohi - hi

(Aarti got a call so she went to the corner. Aarohi walked towards Karan)

Aarohi - what is she doing here

Karan - she ...... is ruining our surprise.

Aarohi - hahaha (mourning like a kid) I feel like killing her. We've planned so much for our Kaira and Kabir

Karan - it's OK. Maybe it's not the right time to do it. And destiny has a different plan for them.

Aarohi - hmm. Maybe

Karan - Btw, you look gorgeous Aaru

Aarohi - thank you. You too, my handsome hunk.

Kabir walked towards Kaira. Kaira was dressed in white, her open hairs were getting tangled. Kaira was about to leave when Kabir had held her hand.

Kaira - umm. ...

Kabir - I'm sorry

Kaira - it's OK

Kabir - I did it all for you. Stay for a while. Please. I mean pleasshhh.

Kaira - (laughed) ok kabiraa, I will only if your Aaru doesn't mind.

Kabir - ah! Forget her. How's the decor.

Kaira - oh! Should I say her that you are planning to forget her? *makes her eyebrows dance*

Kabir - ya ya Go ahead.

Kaira - really! Ok, Aarti (she yells)

Kabir - oh you stop it. (he pulled her

towards him and placed his hands on her lips)

Kaira - mm mm

Kabir - Dr. Psycho! Quite. It's hard for you to get off my grip. (he was happy to hold her in his arms. Smelling her hair which smelled of roses.)

Kaira - (bites his palm) not really

Kabir - ahh. Are you a cat or a human?

Kaira - well, a human though.

Kabir - ahh

Kaira - you okay? Was it painful, let me see (holds his hand)

(Kabir gave away his hands as he knew somewhere that these are the right hands to give away his heart to. He was looking at her with love in his eyes)

Kaira - is it fine (she was blowing over his palm)

Kabir - your breathes are so cold.

Kaira - ik, because I'm feeling cold.

Kabir - hehe, if it was Aarti, she would have made a double meaning out of it.

Kaira - I don't understand double-meaning jokes. (She kept blowing and Kabir was finding it warm)

Kabir - though they are cold your warm hands and their embrace makes it all perfect.

Kaira - hehe, huh! Enough now I'm out of breath, let me get some air.

Kabir - hehe, sure. You didn't say how was the decor.

(Aarti came)

Aarti - oh! I forgot to say that. It's a beautiful baby.

Kabir - well actually, Aarohi did it all.

(Aarti walked towards Karan and Aarohi)

To be continued ....

___

CHAPTER SEVENTEEN

Heart

Once a person regret doing a mistake or is guilty about his doing, forgive him. There is no point in keeping grudges in your heart.

Aarchi Advani Saini.!

Kaira - oh ! Then I should thank Aaru for all this.

Kabir - oh hello , Dr. Psycho it was my idea and I said for pink roses as well you know.

Kaira - oh ! Good

Kabir - just good ?

Kaira - oh my dear kabiraa you are the best. I love the way you apologised to me , loved the decor as well , loved your concern for me etc etc. Enough now flip your short hair !

Kabir - thank you thank you

Kaira - kabiraa, you are really cute !

Kabir - I didn't expect you to forgive me so easily.

Kaira - umm.... I'm not that person. You apologised to me because you are guilty and regret doing what you did. And that's what matters.

Kabir - yeah ! But still. I shouldn't have said all that. I just didn't expect you to say something bad about me.

Kaira - hmm..... I didn't like saying so either but I had to. And if the apology can be this grand then I'll regret not

forgiving you.*giggles*
Kabir - hehehe, your dimples are just ......
Kaira - the cutest ones. I know *flips her hair*
Kabir - a self obsessed psycho.
(They all gathered to have dinner. Karan and Aarohi sat next to each other, holding
their hands under the table. In front where three chairs, Kabir sat in the middle of kaira and Aarti)
Kabir - let's start guys
(Karan and Aarohi served each other)
Kaira - huh ! Couple goals. *giggles*
Aarti - that's really cute to watch them like this.
Kaira - indeed at times , as it's you both , but other than you both , other couple looks cringe.
Kabir - agreed
Aarti - it's not cringe though. And what agreed kabir, even we are a couple.
Kabir - ok let's have food now.
Kaira - (notices kabir while eating) I think the capsicum hates you kabiraa. That's y It's staying out of your plate.
Kabir - I hate capsicum.
Kaira - eat it kabiraa , don't be a picky eater , (picks the capsicum) say aaaaa
Kabir - (opens his mouth)
Kaira - Good boy !
Aarti - baby have this. The mushrooms go really well with the pizza.
Kabir - ah thanks Aarti but I'm allergic to mushrooms. And what's wrong with pizza slice Dr. Psycho
Kaira - my pizza is always toping less. I hate mushrooms , no beef , no extra cheese and no olives.
Kabir - and what's a pizza with less cheese.

Kaira - I like it that way.
Kabir - olives are good for your brain, eat it.
Kaira - ughhh ! Naah
Kabir - eat it Dr. Psycho
Kaira - a stubborn heartless doctor. *makes an expression?*
Kabir - now you say aaaaa
(Karan and Aarohi exchanged a look and smiled at kabir and kaira)

They were just five of them , hanging around and now it was pretty late.
Aarohi - huh ! Fine guys , it was all fun , see you all
Karan - I'll drop you Aaru.
Aarohi - ok hone..... ok Karan
Kaira - did I hear something like ....*winks at Aarohi*
Aarohi - you didn't hear anything. Keep quite.
Kaira - ok now you ppl go me also go.
Kabir - what kind of English is that ?
Kaira - me talk only this way , you don't like it close your ears.
Kabir - you are so annoying
Kaira - *giggles* I know that. Ok tata
Kabir - now what's tata ?
Kaira - *waves her hand* tata bubyeee goodbye wala tata
Kabir - huh ! How will you go
Kaira - walk as always
Kabir - but it's. .....
Kaira - not safe for the person I met bla bla . Just Sssshhhh. I'll go.
Kabir - wait for me downstairs, I'm coming.
Kaira - and what about Aarti

Kabir - I need to talk to her. I hope you will wait for me
Kaira - oh kabiraa , I can wait for you my entire life
giggles
Kabir - So dramatic. Now go maintain the worth of the
word "bye" , I mean tata
Kaira - heheh , okie , tata
Kabir - not again.
(Kaira goes down and kabir walk towards Aarti)
Aarti - kabir, I wanna say you something
Kabir - me to. You say first
Aarti - I think ...... I'm not the right person for you.
Kabir - ummm.... Aarti
Aarti - hmm , I know that you love kaira, I've
seen it in your eyes.
Kabir - I'm confused
Aarti - you needn't need to be. And I'm sorry , I did
hurt you through my words.
Kabir - oh no , it's OK Aaru,
Aarti - now don't wait for anything, get your girl, and
think for a nick name too for her
Kabir - it's already done. Nothings better than 'Dr.
Psycho'
Kabir hugged her
Kabir - I finally got my best fried back
I'm happy.
Aarti - indeed , you did. Now we need to talk to our
parents as well.

Kaira - this kabiraa is taking so long let me see.
(She went upstairs and saw kabir and Aarti together.
She had a weird feeling. Something like losing someone.
She left. Kabir went down but couldn't see her.) The
next day.

Kabir was all delighted to propose his love towards
kaira but. ....
To be continued........

Marriage

Love can either be two-sided or one-sided but things aren't the same in a marriage.

Aarchi Advani Saini.!

But he couldn't find her. He went to ask Aarohi.

Kabir - *knock knock*

Aarohi - come in

Kabir - Dr. Aarohi, do you know where's Dr. Psycho

Aarohi - umm... I think she is in the laboratory, but wait why are you wearing a pink t-shirt today? Ahmm again

Kabir - *blushes* I met the right girl last night and fell for her

Aarohi - oh my! Dr. Kabir! You and romantic. Weird combination

Kabir - Ummm. ..... can be a deadly one to

Aarohi - *giggles* go and get your girl. I'm glad to see that you found the right one finally.

Kabir - finally?¿¿

Aarohi - hmm.....me and Karan thought about it already

Kabir - thought about what?

Aarohi - you and Kaira of course. Somewhere we felt that you both are made for each other and Aarti isn't right for you.

Kabir - hmm. But you both never said

Aarohi - we thought of but love can be one-sided and you and Aarti are getting married and marriage needs to be both-sided. The decision should be taken by both of the individuals.

Kabir - hmm, you are right. I need to talk to Kaira about it.

Kabir walked towards the laboratory and saw her. She was dressed in a pink Kurti embroidered with white flowers and a white dupatta hanging to her side shoulder. Hairs tied up in a half-tie hairstyle. Eyes hazel brown and lips cherry kissed. Kabir was lost. Starring at her.

Karan - Bro! Wassup! Why are you looking at her in a daze?

Kabir - oh! You scared me! Nothing!

Karan - bro you can share.

Kabir - you know, Dr. Psycho is Cute. I've started loving her. These days I had to remind myself that I'm engaged. I like Aarti. She is my best friend, but I never loved her. Our marriage was fixed by our parents as Mom wanted us to get married.

Karan - hmm...Indeed I agree with the fact that she is Cute. But Bro, please I like her, you have Aarti na, keep her, leave her for me. (He teases him to see his reaction)

Kabir - (eye rolls at him) I thought about her first. And you have Aarohi.

Karan - Bro! No! I know her first!

Kabir - I saw her first! I won!

Karan - broooohhh! You can't do this. Aarti won't spare you. Hehehe, Kaira influenced you, Bro. Even you started to win arguments.

Kabir - I already had a conversation with Aarti and she herself said me to express my love for Kaira

Karan - really! That's so sweet of her Bro! Are you okay? You seem stressed.
Kabir - I am Karan. Love can be both one-sided and two-sided, but marriage! I need to know what Kaira feels before I talk to mom about us. I have a plan.
Karan - spill it, Bro! I will help you. Anything for you.
Kabir - ok listen

———————

Kabir was under weird emotions. He is surprised to know how can Kaira have such an impact on him. Karan spoke to Kaira about it. He said that Kabir is confused about his relationship with Aarti and said that he is a bit worried and under stress. Kaira was worried about Kabir.
Kaira - how's that possible Karan, last night I saw them together and they were happy.
Karan - sometimes things appear to be like that, but that isn't the reality.
Kaira - I didn't get you
Karan - sometimes you see something and assume an opinion, but that's not the right thing. Maybe what you saw wasn't the way you were supposed to see. Get it. But Bro was really stressed. I'm worried about him.
Kaira - hmmm. I'll talk to you later Karan.
She was attending to her patient. She was distracted.
Patient - Dr. Kaira I feel worried for no reason.
Kaira - I know right, me too. Though I don't have any feelings for Kabir still I'm worried about him. Or I do have feelings. Last night I don't know why, I felt weird when he was with Aarti
Patient - haann??¿¿
Kaira - oh! Nothing! What else?
Patient - my mind goes numb and I can't sleep.
Kaira - So me. Even I'm facing this.

Patient - ??¿¿¿*confused*
Kaira - wait. I'll attend to you soon
Patient - doctor, doctor!!!!!
Kaira takes a taxi.
Kaira calls Karan
Karan - yes Kaira
Kaira - Karan! Tell me exactly where Kabir is or probably where he can be
Karan - he visits the central park often when he is stressed. Might be there
Kaira - uh ok.
She calls Kabir, but he didn't receive her call.
Kaira noticed the number plate of a car and stops the taxi. The car had hit his bumper to the trunk of a tree.
Kaira - that's Kabir's car (she screams)
A crowd gathered there and Kaira passes through it and reaches the door and ....
To be continued ....

CHAPTER NINETEEN

Fears

At times the fear of falling in love is the biggest of all fears.
Aarchi Advani Saini.!
And she didn't find him there.
Kaira - Kabir, (she screams)
She fell to the ground screaming his name when tears
started rolling down her cheeks. Only when she felt
someone's hand on her shoulder. She turns back and saw
him, Kabir perfectly fine.
Kaira - kabiraa, you are here (Her eyes filled with tears,
but her lips curled into a smile when she saw him. She
hugged him
tight)
Kabir - yes, I'm here always here, and always by your
side. (Kabir wrapped his arms around her waist and rested
his chin on her head)
Kaira - (came off his arms and agitated her hands on his
chest) I hate you. ..... I hate you. .....I hate you !!!! Do you
have any idea how badly you scared me? (Tears started
rolling down again)
Kabir - (Wipes her tears) I'm sorry Dr. Psycho
Kaira - I hate you but I love you
Kabir - I hate you too and I love you the most.

She again sneaked into his arms and synced her beats
with his.
Winds were blowing and Kaira's hair fell upon her face.
Kabir tucked the strands behind her tiny and red ears. Her
closed eyelids and lashes dipped in tears weren't
less than an oyster enclosing a pearl. He kissed her
forehead.
Kaira felt safe there, and anyone will. But Kaira left his
arms.
Kabir - what happened
Kaira - I don't love you
Kabir - your statement can't change the words in your
eyes.
Kaira - stop reading my eyes, Kabir. It's all fake. Don't
trust them. They are all a facade.
Kabir - such deep dialogues, don't suit you psycho!
Kaira - I don't believe in love Kabir.
Kabir - I'll make you believe it.
Kaira - I'm scared to love and there are many things I'm
scared of. You haven't seen that Kaira.
Kabir - list your fears.
Kaira - what
Kabir - I said list your fears
Kaira - many fears. Fear of crowd, fear of darkness, fear
of heights, fear of touch, fear of love, fear of speed, and
fear of losing ppl I love.
Kabir - ok so, I'll be holding your hand when you pass a
crowd, I'll be your bodyguard so that nobody dares to
touch you other than me, I'll be by your side in darkness
so that you aren't scared, I won't ever let you stand on
heights, I'll never drive at high speed, I'll never betray you
and never leave you.

Kaira - no Kabir, I can't snatch you from Aarti. Your family had already set it all.

Kabir - I spoke......

Kaira - no! I can't hurt her ..... I've hurt ppl enough (she started taking her steps back)

Kabir - Kaira! Listen to me. Kaira stop

Kaira turned and walked away. She went to the hospital and shuts the door of her cabin. An envelope slides inside her cabin

and touches her feet.

-Dear Dr. Psycho

No matter how much you deny I know you love me, and no matter how much you ignore you will find love for me in my eyes. Maybe destiny has set different paths for us. Maybe we were just supposed to meet but not be together like the moon and the stars. Every night they meet but they are never together, or maybe they are. I won't force you if it's a no. But remember if not you then no one else ...... no one. I can marry Aarti for the sake of my parents, but remember you were my first love and the last one too. And maybe these khaadhos of yours will always remain loveless or maybe loverless. I loved you, I still love you and I will always love you. I wanna see you happy that's all. I've never wished good luck to ppl or never thought of their

happiness but I do care about yours. Stay happy!

- LOVE YOU DR. PSYCHO! -

Warm tears started rolling down her cheeks. Her cheeks were all red and Kabir could see it all through the window.

Kaira - *whispered* I love you to my khaadhos!

———————————————————

The next day Mrs. Sinha came to Kaira's cabin.

Mrs. Sinha - hello my dear

Kaira - oh! Hello Mrs. Sinha. How are you?

Mrs. Sinha - I'm fine, How are you, my dear?

Kaira - I'm fine to

Mrs. Sinha - but I don't feel like you are fine.

Kaira - don't worry Mrs. Sinha. I'm alright

Mrs. Sinha - ok if you say so, anyway, I bought a gift for you

Kaira - for me, but why Mrs. Sinha

Mrs. Sinha - what why? You bought me and Kabir in a bond which I never had. This is just nothing Infront of it.

(Tears sneaked out)

To be continued.......

CHAPTER TWENTY

Wedding

Best friends are never invited to a wedding, they are already a part of it. Love always comes along with a touch of possessiveness.
Aarchi Advani Saini.!
Kaira - oh my dearest madam, you are so emotional just like my maa, I understand
Mrs. Sinha - I bought one for Aarohi and one for you, a lehnga.
Kaira - oh! But why for her and why a lehnga for me.
Mrs. Sinha - oh! She didn't say you. Aarohi is getting engaged to my son.
Kaira - really! She didn't say me. I swear I won't spare her.
Mrs. Sinha - ok ok don't get angry m dear, look at this
(A brightly colored obviously pink lehenga with tons of bright laces and finishing. I'm bad at describing clothes ?)
Kaira - Woah! It's boottiiffuulll Mrs. Sinha. …. ah…I mean it's beautiful
Mrs. Sinha - really! I'm glad you loved it! Keep it boottiiffuulll
Kaira - *giggles*
Mrs. Sinha - ok so you have to attend the engagement today ok, and Wear this

Kaira - sure Mrs. Sinha. A best friend is never Invited to a wedding, she is a part of
it. I'll be there.
(Mrs. Sinha leaves and Kaira walks towards Aarohi's cabin)
Kaira - Aaru
Aarohi - *busy typing* yeah! *hides her phone*
Kaira - how dare you
Aarohi - what happened
Kaira - huh!!!!! *started mourning like a child*
Aarohi - what's wrong baby
Kaira - your baby is dead
Aarohi - but you here, right in front of me.
Kaira - you are getting engaged and you didn't say me. I hate you
Aarohi - uh, I forgot. And anyway I'm marrying the one you love.
Kaira - yeap, obviously Karan , I like him for you
Aarohi - hmm *busy texting*
Kaira - whom are you talking to *sneaks in*
Aarohi - *hides the phone* Kabir
Kaira - Kabir ?¿my Kabir
Aarohi - if you wanna be psychotically possessive about another human being, than yes, your Kabir
Kaira - I'm not being psychotic. What are you talking
Aarohi - nothing about you and not your concern.
Kaira - why are you being rude to me.
Aarohi - he said he loves you and you said no, though you love him
Kaira - uhh! Aaru yaar. Ok how's your lehnga
Aarohi - hmm hmm, change the topic. Make vain attempts
Kaira - I'll see you tonight, I'll dress you up.

Aarohi - Aarti is gonna do that. You dress up nicely, I want my bestie to rock in her wedding. ..... I mean in my wedding
Kaira - ok then it's not my fault if all eyes are on me and not you
Aarohi - I won't mind, now go

The bright pink lehnga contrasted with Kaira's fair complexion. Her curly hairs, jhumkas, and mehndi were all perfect. Her lashes curled up in mascara, eyes That are beautiful enough and pink lips made her look like a princess.
She walked into the venue hall and saw the stage. There was her mum too.
Kaira - maa, you said me you are busy, you won't come.
Kaira's mom - oh I did. But you have to come if it's your daughter's engagement
Kaira - hain ??
Maa - I mean Aarohi of course, she is not less than a daughter to me.
Kaira - hmm. You look pretty though maa.
Maa - thank you bacha!
Kaira went on the stage to meet Aarohi
Kaira - woohoo, look at you. My goodness, you like a goddess. We have the same design, just different colours.
Aarohi - thank you, baby, you too. Ufff the looks and hairstyle, and mines are red and yours as expected nothing other than pink.
Kaira - hehe, you know me
Kabir walked in with Karan by his side. Both wearing the same suit. A black blazer with a white neat shirt inside, well tucked in, hairs all set and beard all trimmed.
Kaira - *looks away*

Aarohi - what's wrong look at him, he's looking at you
Kaira - I can't. He is making me fall for him.
Kabir saw Kaira and his lips curled into a smile, his cute dimples popped on the side of his cheeks.
Kabir - *cleared his throat*
Kaira - hi Karan, you look handsome.
Karan - thanks Kaira! You too, I mean, Bro wasn't getting his eyes off you
Kabir - *stamped his feet*
Karan - aah !!
Mrs. Sinha - ok now times running. Kabir makes Aarohi wear the ring.
Kaira - wait! Aarohi
Mrs. Sinha - ya! Aarohi
Aarohi - ya me. I said to you I'm marrying someone you love
Kabir - yes Aaru, ok give me your hand Aarohi
Kaira - wait! What! But Karan, you
Karan - what Kaira
Kaira - Kabir, how can you marry Aarohi
Kabir - if I can't marry you then I'll marry her
Kaira - what the.....
To be continued ....

CHAPTER TWENTY-ONE

Hugs

Hate is just another form of love that didn't get a chance to express itself logically, hate, hugs, amour, till eternity.
Aarchi Advani Saini.!
Kaira - that doesn't make any sense.
Kabir - it does. I want to marry you but you don't wanna marry me. I don't wanna marry Aarti, so I'll marry Aarohi. Simple.
Kaira - what simple, have you lost it. And you Aaru, what's wrong with you
Aarohi - nothing. He said he wants to marry me I said yes. He did say you that he loves you. But you ignored him.
Kaira - you ppl have lost it all, have you gone nuts kabir
Mrs. Sinha - we are running out of time. Kabir , son , make the right girl wear the ring .
Kabir - yes mom
Kaira - what right , there's no right , there's no left. ....
Kabir - you ssshh *placed his finger on his lips*
Kabir takes up kaira's hand in his and places the ring on the right finger.
(Everybody laughed)
Kaira - what was this.....
Kaira's mom - you keep pranking ppl , we pranked you. And remember you said me that you'll marry the guy I'll

choose for you, this is it. I've chosen kabir for you.

Kaira - ah....uh...wait....ah

Kabir - let me clear it. I said Mom already about you and Aarti as well. They both were ok with the fact that I love you. Then I asked mom to talk to your mum just the way you like marriage proposals to be. Me ,Aarohi and karan have set this plan.

Kaira - *blushes and looks away* how do you know I like marriage proposals to be this way?

Kabir - Aarohi said me

Aarohi - I'm sorry for hiding it. But you didn't leave us with any choice.

Kaira - isshh okieee

Mrs. Sinha - oh now , karan it's your turn.

Karan makes Aarohi wear the ring. Everybody stood for a family photo. Kabir and Kaira standing together, karan and Aarohi also together. The couples were in the middle and their families on the side.

Kabir - you look gorgeous Dr.Psycho

Kaira - thenkuuu kabiraa, you look Dayummmmmm

Kabir - how was it

Kaira - (eyes getting filled with tears) I don't know !

Kabir - oh you! Save some tears for the last moment with your mum. *Wipes her tears and hugs her*

Kaira - I hate you

Kabir - uh , I was expecting the three magical words.

Kaira - hate is more intense than love and just another form of love. And for me hate is 'hugs , amour till eternity'

Kabir - oh ! That's nice , then be in my arms forever.

Kaira - ok stop it now ! Everyone's looking at us. What will they say

Kabir - they'll say that look at him , he is so in love with her , but she ....

Kaira - hehehe, but she loves him more.

Finally , it's wedding time. Both The brides and the grooms are ready. They've taken their vows and all set to begin a new life with each other.

Kaira - I'll missh you maa

Maam - ok ok stop it

Kaira - huh ! You are not even crying

Kabir - why will she. She's getting rid of you. She is supposed to celebrate! Right maa

Maa - of course son

Kaira - hey you khadhoos, stop influencing my maa

Maa - how can you call your husband, khaadhos! Say Sorry

Kaira - sorry khaadhos ! But maa , really ? You won't miss me

Maa - my bacha I will ! But kabir has shifted our place to a new house next to the Sinha mansion.

Kaira - what?

Maa - hmm.....

Kabir - maa can't live All alone after you leave come along with me , so I thought of shifting your old home near our place.

Kaira - thank you Kabir

Kabir - keep it thenkuuu, I like it that way. It's OK.

Mrs. Sinha - I never thought that both my sons will marry on the same day.

Kaira - and I never thought that my bestie will be my co - sister

Aarohi - hehe , me to

Karan - that's nice , we won't have dramatic fights. Isn't it Bro

Kabir - hmm , can't say. Where there is Dr. Psycho,
drama comes along.
Everybody laughed and cried.

Kaira reached kabir's room. Walls painted in grey and
blue. A picture of him hanging above the bed. A study
table on the corner. A simple and descent room.
Kaira changed her dress and started eating. Kabir
entered.
Kabir - don't you get tired of wearing so
much of pink
Kaira - what's wrong with pink and room , doesn't have
anything which is pink, it seems like I don't belong here.
Kabir - indeed you don't belong here coz you live here
(places his hand on his heart)
To be continued......

CHAPTER TWENTY-TWO

Unintentionally

Few love stories have a beautiful journey, some got over and some stayes, trust me all are full of miracles you'll surely find someone who loves you truely, madely, and unintentionally.

Aarchi Advani Saini.!

Kaira - oh! You cheesy homo sapien, just Ssshhh

Kabir - and what are you eating

Kaira - strawberries

Kabir - why ?

Kaira - because I'm starving. There was nothing in your fridge, other than strawberries and apples.

Kabir - haven't you eaten in the wedding hall

Kaira - you expect me to eat. Huhhhh ! Do you now how decently brides are supposed to behave. You can't fill your plate completely, after every bite your mouth is wiped, and the bites this small, this tiny. How will my tummy feel satisfied.

Kabir - I feel sad for you

Kaira - *bites her strawberry*, you better feel it

Kabir - ok now come with me

Kabir and kaira sneaks inside the kitchen.

Kabir - couples come home after there wedding and enjoy their first night , and we

are....
Kaira - *eating raw noodles* what were you saying
Kabir - nothing and what are you eating
Kaira - I'm making Maggi
Kabir - no wonder you are insane
Kaira - I know that
Kaira wearing her pink night suit all set to own kabir's heart. Her hairs all falling over her cheekbones.
Kabir - *wraps his arms around her waist* I've waited for this moment, for so long
Kaira - you don't leave a chance to hold me around yourself.
Kabir - na , and I've never planned such a first night.
Kaira - hehehe , ssshhh. Let's eat.
(They went to there rooms and started eating)
Kabir - is that how you eat noodles
Kaira - yup , like this
Kabir takes his phone and records it
Kaira - why are you recording it. Ugh ! I look disgusting
Kabir - no you don't! And if you ever scold my kids for eating in a messy manner , I'll show this to them , and say your mum also did this.
Kaira - hehehe, ha ha show it.
Kabir - now ?
Kaira - *yawns* now sleeping time. You don't have any idea how tired I'm. Standing on the stage , wearing such a heavy lehnga and so much jewellery, meeting all the guests etc etc. I'm exhausted. I've planned so much for our first night but my head is aching, now give me a head massage
Kabir - ????
Kaira - heheh , don't make that expression, you look funny
Kabir - ok ok

Kaira leans on her pillow, in a sitting
manner closes her eyes and kabir rubs her head in a
hypnotically relaxing rhythm.
Kaira - uhh ! Ahh . Ya keep doing it. It feels peace.
Kaira Opens her eyes and looks at kabir. His eyes
dwelling in hers , his fingers across her forehead , his
cheeks turning red and lips curling into a smile.
Kaira - ok now control your desires.
Kabir - now you ssshh. Finger on your lips.
Kaira - *places her finger on her lips*
Kabir - what do you think of yourself, haan , do you
know how many nights I have spend here wishing for your
presence and now when you are hear you
Kaira - ya but
Kabir - I said finger on your lips, what does that mean?
Kaira - you asked me to place my finger on my lips, you
didn't ask me to be quite. Two different statements kabiraa
Kabir - ok then I'll keep you quite in another way
Kaira - which. ....
Before kaira could say anything, Kabir had pressed his
lips against hers. Kaira closes her eyes
Kabir - this way
Kaira - oh ! I like the way
LIGHTS OFF

The next morning, na , actually a perfect morning kaira
opened her eyes and saw kabir. She was all in her arms and
she felt blessed to have him.
Kabir - stop staring me
Dr. Psycho
Kaira - you are awake
Kabir - before you. I wanted to see you while you were
sleeping and wanted to be the first to open my eyes and

see you with me , all in my arms. (Hugs kaira)
Kaira - I love you
Kabir - oh wait , did I hear that
Kaira - ok now don't be dramatic
Kabir - always less than you. Repeat please. .... I mean
pleasshhh
Kaira - I ...... love ...... you
Kabir - again
Kaira - *kisses his forehead* I love you
Kabir - haye , I love you to
Dr. Psycho !

HAPPIES ENDINGS ♥♥

---

www.ingramcontent.com/pod-product-compliance
Lightning Source LLC
Chambersburg PA
CBHW031356160726
47993CB00002B/1004